Kittycat Lullaby

EILEEN SPINELLI

ILLUSTRATED BY ANNE MORTIMER

HYPERION BOOKS FOR CHILDREN • NEW YORK

Printed in Singapore

This book is set in 22-point Goudy Oldstyle Bold.

The artwork for each picture was prepared using watercolor.

First Edition
1 3 5 7 9 10 8 6 4 2

LIBRARY OF CONGRESS CATALOGING-IN-PUBLICATION DATA
Spinelli, Eileen.
Kittycat lullaby / Eileen Spinelli ; illustrated by Anne Mortimer.—1st ed.
p.   cm.
Summary: Having had a busy day, Kittycat settles down to purr a drowsy purr and go to sleep.
ISBN 0-7868-0458-0 (trade)
[1. Cats—Fiction. 2. Bedtime—Fiction. 3. Stories in rhyme.]
I. Mortimer, Anne, ill. II.
Title.
PZ8.3.S759Ki 2001
[E]—dc21 00-31901

Visit www.hyperionchildrensbooks.com

*H*ush-a-bye, Kittycat
Such a busy day
Dancing after rainbows
Scaring mice away

Hiding in the tall grass
Scratching at the door

*S*watting yellow yarn balls
'Round the playroom floor

*S*niffing pots of catmint

Prancing on the chairs

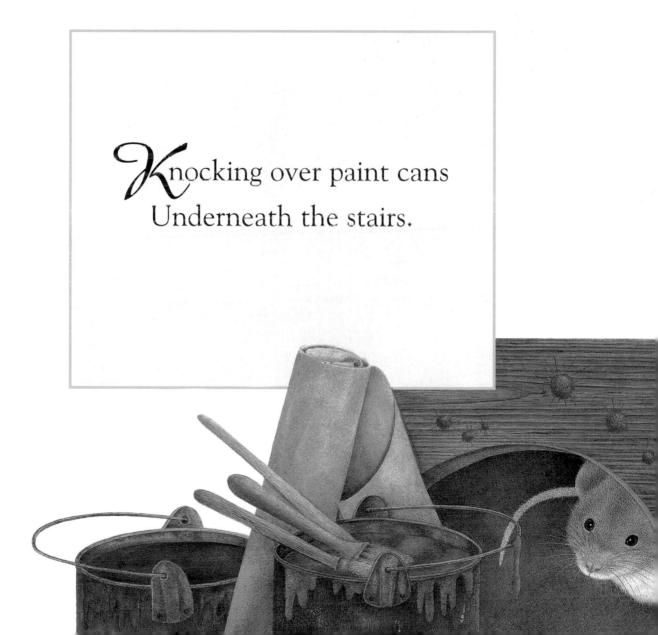

*K*nocking over paint cans
Underneath the stairs.

*H*ush-a-bye, Kittycat
Shadows sail through town
Time to wash your whiskers
Time to settle down

Climb into your basket
With that tattered sock
Listen to the ticking
of the kitchen clock

Smile your cozy cat grin
Purr your drowsy purr
Snuggle as the bright moon
Dapples down your fur.

*H*ush-a-bye, Kittycat

Stars shine there for you

Holding secret wishes

Yours just might

come true

Should you have a bad dream
I will be nearby
Close enough to hold you
If I hear you cry.

Close your sleepy eyes, now—
I'll turn off the light—
See you in the morning
Kittycat, good night!